Cover: Denis Vierge
Graphic design (series)*:* Lili Fleury

For Jules, Samaelle,Carlota and Joachim,
for their kind.

Series "Illustrated Tales for Adults"

◆◆◆

BRAIDS

◆◆◆

In the series "Illustrated Tales for Adults," contemporary writers explore the most recent research in sciences through fiction, reviving a tradition in scientific literature – as Lewis Carroll did in his time. A tradition that encourages readers to dream and meditate on the way the world is represented as it redefines itself today.

www.disvoir.com/an/ls/a/9_14_0.html

in the same series

THEORY OF MULTIDREAMS

A Cosmic-Dream Investigation by H.P. Lovecraft

with Jean-Philippe Cazier (writer), Andreas Marchal (illustrator), inspired by astrophysicist Aurélien Barrau's work on "Multiverses".

THE ADVENTURES OF PERCIVAL

A Phylogenetic Tale

with Pierres Senges (writer), Nicolas de Crecy (illustrator) inspired by the works of Dominique Lestel (philosopher-ethologist) based on the phylogenetic classification of the living: a new vision on evolutionary relationships and sociality between Human/Animal.

THE MANWHO REFUSED TO DIE

with Nicolas Ancion (writer), Patrice Killoffer (illustrator), inspired by the works of François Taddei (geneticist) on the bacterium Escherichia and Immortality.

BRAIDS
MEMORIES OF THE NARRATOCENE

by Léo Henry

illustrated by Denis Vierge

with the participation of
Hervé Le Guyader

series directed by
Daniele Riviere

"There is no mistake, just as there is no death. There can be no mistake. Our imagination, even during sleep, even in madness, can create realities – indisputable, strong, powerful and concrete realities."

- Jean Cassou, on Jean Painlevé's films, 1931.

The texts in *Braids, Memories of the Narratocene* date from around the year zero. They are considered to be one of the last written testimonies of *Homo sapiens* as a unique human species.

We propose here a translation of the most complete version known, found in the memory pits of Bayan Obo. The poetic quirks have been preserved.

We have long stopped pretending that we were capable of understanding everything.

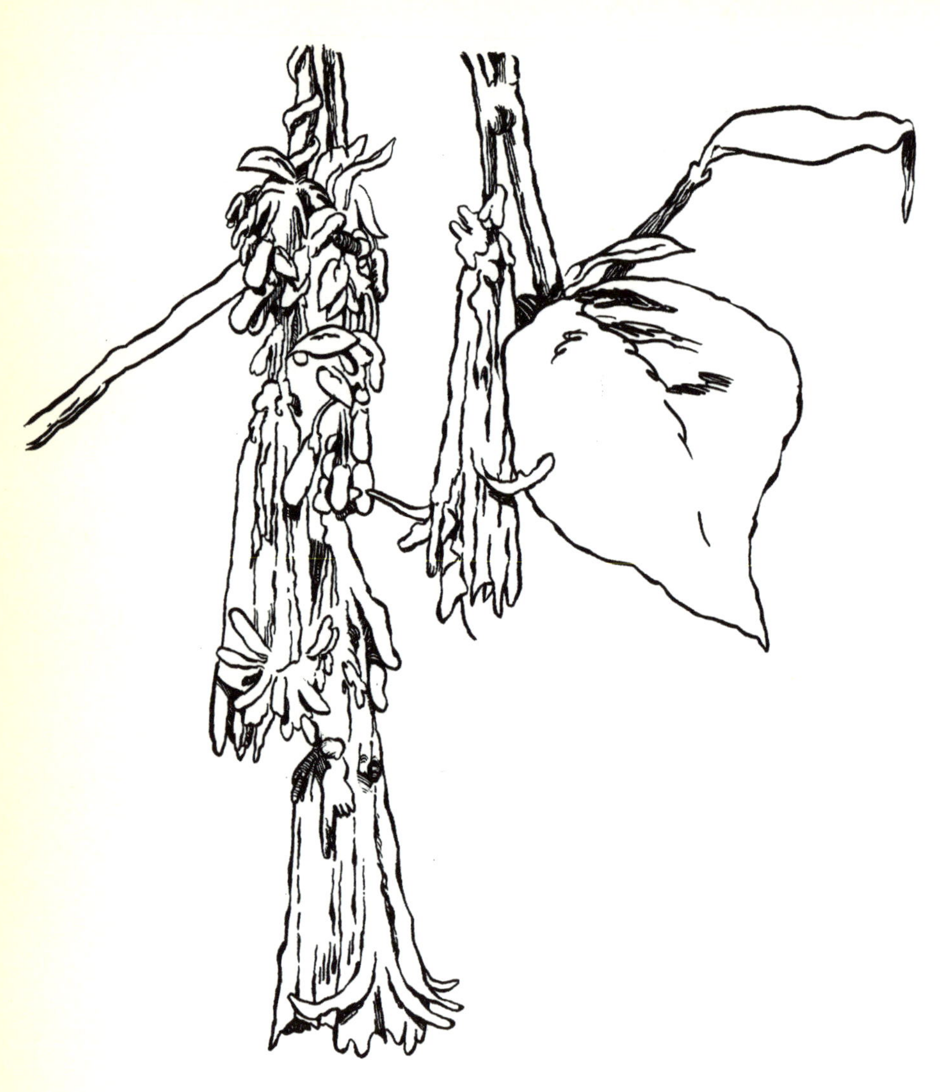

THE EXPEDITION

THE ISLAND

The island frightened me first.

I didn't like its abrupt appearance or its smells. During the day, it was warmer than in the Greenhouses or on the boat and the wind kept changing power and direction. The very air in which I was moving passed over my skin like a nasty caress. "This world stinks," I thought, only moments after I set foot on land. And this intuition carried all the fear of the Outside conveyed by my culture and all our love for order and tidiness, which had allowed us to survive a century and a half of disasters.

Of course, I had volunteered for the expedition, and my application for this position as librarian had only been selected after a rigorous recruitment process. An assembly of +2 had scrutinized my profile, and I had only reached this part of the world because I had been judged the right woman for this cultural collection mission.

The trip had felt long and oppressive, but our flawless organization had overcome all the bad experiences. We had faced two tropical storms with no loss of life and little material damage, and the entire crew had withstood the twenty-two days of sailing without appearing upset by the shock of strangeness. I must admit that the setting did not feel too unfamiliar: the ship's living space was as confined as that of our cells, and our working constraints were even stricter than in the Greenhouse.

The vastness of the ocean and sky was reduced to well-ordered abstract visions, in which we knew that nothing threatened to tip us over. The stars, at night, were in exactly the same place as those in our projections and illustrations. The trade winds blew steadily and carried only the pungent smell of salt. Only my first rainstorm caught me unawares: this rain that everyone kept talking about was not that different from the artificial rain in our domes, and even though the drops fell from the whole height of the sky, they felt no heavier than water from a shower. In fact, it was only when the island came into sight that I really felt the fear of the Outside.

Its silhouette became more and more complex, more and more steep as we approached. The ruined port was drowned in vegetation of unexpected colours, itself overflown by a jumble of wild birds. Fortunately, the docking manoeuvres required all our attention until dawn, and without discussion we gave up on establishing a bivouac ashore.

The swing of my ship, so unpleasant for the past three weeks, felt attenuated by the proximity of the land, and this worried me. As I could not sleep, I went out on the deck and discovered, in the darkness of the heights, a red glow, pulsating like the heart of a dissected mouse. The word volcano was not unknown to me and I had known from the beginning what my destination would be. Until then, however, I had not understood this word.

We were brought together in pairs, each in charge of supporting and monitoring the other. We were given maps of the conurbation, which were to be updated as we progressed. Then the operating crews went ashore.

I had imagined many times this reunion with the world of the past - my excitement as a pioneer, my humility as a researcher, my concern as a citizen. We often talked about wars, epidemics and famines. Outside was a mythical theatre of all hostilities, the justification for our relentless rules and deprivations. I was astounded by the calm that reigned there, by the heady power of the fragrances and the vital, tiny, perpetual swarming of the landscapes.

Our first days were spent clearing traffic lanes between the ruins of low-rise buildings, inventorying the main materials to be collected. Depending on the final resources and manpower at our disposal, these would be extracted later, stored on the shore and then loaded onto the barges.

We encountered no trace of intelligent life, as if everything, except the inert matter, had eventually dissolved into the humid air. The corpses themselves, those of the mass graves whose images we had seen again and again in our history classes, had long disappeared. Insects, fungi and moulds ruled a kingdom of climbing plants, thorny bushes and large gnarled trees. At the chapter reviewing the first dozen days, I reported on the failure of my mission: there was not a single book in the conurbation.

Resource exploitation began while some scouts continued to update the maps, paddling from point to point, barely venturing into the coastal forests. I was tasked with sorting copper with my +0. We would split the pipes open, pull out the cables and carefully strip the metal, and I was satisfied with this physically painful and intellectually monotonous task that kept my concern at bay. Then I was called in to share my thoughts about my situation.

"I am surprised at the absence of any written material, I said. There are only a few toponymic signs, old posters, hate graffiti and security instructions. But reports and testimonies, just like scholarly and entertainment books, all seem to have disappeared.

- Nothing else?"

I thought about it and then added:

"I didn't find any radio receiver either, whether complete or in pieces. And yet electronic scrap is very common."

We were still sleeping on board the boats, but they seemed more impregnated every day with the warm and organic smell of the island. Before unlocking the cabin doors, we had to chase the increasingly daring seabirds off the decks. A veil of orange seaweed was setting on the hulls where the waves came to beat. I dreamed, I believed I had woken up in the common dormitory where I had spent my youth. In the morning, I learned that I had been assigned a new task.

"What is expected of me?

- We discovered where the radios are, my +1 informed me. The books are probably in the same area."

He pointed to a very distant geographical point on my map, almost at the centre of the island and in the extreme heights, which had been triangulated by the scanners.

“Take the equipment you need from the commissary and come back in two dozen at the latest.”

THE VOLCANO

The ascent took me two days.

As none of our vehicles could facilitate my progress, I had loaded myself heavily and moved forward with excessive caution in this unknown territory. Before the end of the first hour of walking, I found myself alone for the first time in my life. There was no trace of artefacts, no more constructions, no walls to stop the gaze, no measuring or environmental control equipment. Not even the proximity of a familiar body, the echo of a human voice. My receiver was continuously spitting out static sounds, my last connection to my community.

The Outside world assumed a new, unthinkable and totally savage face. There were only plants and animals, thick red earth, rough black stones: a gigantic and stupid conglomerate of matter to which I understood nothing, in which I could hardly make out any singularities or name anything. Most of the trees had similarities with the species in my Greenhouse or with images computed from the databases, but these impressions of familiarity did not stand up to scrutiny. As soon as I tried to identify a particular variety, I failed to isolate an individual from its neighbour or the latter from the surrounding trees, or to tell a plant apart from the lichens, parasitic species, fungi, animal droppings and insects that lived in it. It was as if all the biotopes of all the existing Greenhouses in the world had been gathered before my eyes and mixed in an absolute mess. And it continued, it proliferated all along my path, subtly changing its appearance, giving an impression of chaos without beginning or end.

Seen from afar, the island had seemed threatening to me. From up close, it became unreadable and crazy, and the discomfort I felt at that moment had something to do with the intoxication, the nausea of letting go. I thought I understood why the humans condemned to remain outside the Greenhouses had eventually perished: the Outside world was so senseless that its spectacle alone undermined your reason.

But I had been given a mission, I had orders and kept moving forward. At the end of the first day, I emerged from the forest and walked on a wide and winding path: the trace of a path built during the age of concrete, or the transhumance path of a large mammal species. Down below, the sea turned metal grey but a fold of ground hid the ships from me. Behind my back, I felt the mass of the mountain, its sides like giant partitions, velvety with vegetation. A waterfall roared, invisible. I had dinner, unfolded my cocoon and slept for eight hours without a dream.

I resumed my journey in the morning, entered a narrow gorge and found myself walking on an escarpment as wide as two palms, between a steep incline and a cliff. The map confirmed that I was moving in the right direction. The slope became weaker, the path winding between the rocky massifs with a form of intelligence that clearly seemed to reveal human intention. Thinking beings had designed this path to penetrate this oversized circus. Despite the flora, the small fauna, the vastness of the environment and the chaos of stimuli, I was beginning to feel a form of relief. My feet had found a way. I was putting my steps in other people's steps. I was no longer quite alone in the wilderness.

I walked forward until I was hungry, sat on a rock for a snack, but jumped back on my feet when I saw the dogs. There were three of them: two large, one smaller, with short yellow-brown hairs and bright black eyes. They had approached me quietly while I was eating and had stopped at a cautious distance, standing in line a few meters away, to examine me without hostility.

Two archive images were fighting inside me: that of the primitive man, bare-chested, wearing a leather loincloth and accompanied by his most faithful companion, and an urban guerrilla video in which hordes of chipped and harnessed fighting dogs snarled at fractious rioters to disperse them. I had no experience of an animal of this size, muscular and armed with fangs, so I just froze and waited.

The smallest of the dogs eventually broke away from the group and approached me. It passed me without a look, although I held out a bite of meat pudding in my open hand. And when I finally got back on the road, I realized that it had simply gone behind me to bring up the rear. The two big ones came before me and the last one followed, matching my own pace: a stoic escort that reacted neither to my calls nor to my pretending to throw stones at them.

The second day was well underway when, after climbing up a series of very steep gorges with traces of stairs carved into the rock, I reached the cultivated plateau. Then I heard the dogs barking for the first time, and the sound they produced was only remotely similar to the one I associated with the cries of their species. It was less powerful, more strangled and loaded with unexpected highs. The leading animals were communicating with a peer out of sight in what sounded like an excited dialogue. Out of breath, I climbed the steep path, leaning with my hands against the close-set walls, and I burst into the village.

The dogs were greeting the two-legged creature with whom they had been conversing. They interrupted their game when they saw me, and three pairs of eyes turned toward me. Astounded, I then realized that this being was a human female with a shock of grey hair. She bared her teeth and growled in my direction.

THE TRIBE

The inhabitants of the plateau welcomed me with benevolent indifference and allowed me to stay with them for the twenty days of my expedition. They belonged to a remarkable looking variety, and their behaviour could shift so dramatically that I often mistook one for the other during the first dozen. I was never able to determine their exact number, although I believe there must have been almost a hundred of them, not to mention the animals with which they lived without fences.

The first two days passed in the greatest confusion. The humans on the plateau ignored me, behaved like animals, sent me to eat with the pigs and spend the night with the dogs. They touched me, sniffed me, took interest in the buckles of my shoes, then returned to acting as if I didn't exist.

During the second night, heavy rains broke out. The walls of my cocoon, which I had unfolded at the edge of the village, broke under the pressure of the rain. I ran for shelter into a hut, usually occupied by three women, their cats and a large grey bird. No one paid the slightest attention when I arrived, except for one of the tomcats that, at dawn, came to enjoy the warmth of my blanket. The sun was rising when I finally fell asleep. When I woke up, one of the women was curled up against me. I first tried to smile at her without success, then I got up a little suddenly, feeling uncomfortable.

I quickly found what I had come looking for: two kinds of hangars, long buildings without windows, had been built on the wooded hill overlooking the village. They served as a repository for an impressive array of electronics and shelves filled with thousands of tight volumes. A water mill, upstream of the irrigation canals, also supplied electricity to a rather complex radio system and a series of reading lamps. There was even a device with a screen that I identified as an archaic computer terminal, in apparent working order.

The books were all old, some very degraded despite the obvious care with which they were preserved. I did not understand how they were classified. It was obvious that someone had established an order there, but it remained elusive to me. I found no copies or documents, handwritten or printed, which could have been produced after the major epidemics.

Until the fourth evening of my stay, when a child spoke to me in my own language, I convinced myself that the members of this tribe had regressed to a pre-civilized stage, living with their animals in a form of stupid animality. They ate with them, whether sitting, squatting or crawling. Adults played with pigs as we used to as children with fellow unit members. The few human interactions I observed reminded me of documents I had seen on the great apes. What I had read about the disasters that hit the Outside had made a strong enough impression on me: I had no doubt that their behaviours were the direct consequence of these events. It never occurred to me that if the villagers were behaving like animals, it was because they had acquired the opportunity, or even the privilege, to do so.

The library hangars were not the only functional technological facilities on the plateau. At the boundary between the very ingeniously irrigated fields and orchards, I discovered a smokehouse and a cooler refrigerated by a system of wind turbines. A large oval solar oven served as a hearth for dozens of hollow containers, carved from fruit varieties. The work at these different posts, such as hunting, fishing or gathering food, appeared to be of minor concern to the locals, who were more impatient to roll on the ground with a dog or to wade dreamily through an irrigation canal.

It was this lightness with which they considered their own survival that I considered the most bestial. I could not see any hierarchy among them. Only the children, whether human or not, appeared to be the object of specific care. For the rest, everyone commerced with everyone else on an equal footing, barked, growled, chatted or kept quiet until I was with them, or went on with their lives as if I was not there.

I spent the first few days of my stay consulting the books they were storing. They were mostly written in languages I had studied, and I flashed page after page of those that seemed most precious to me. I also listened to their radio, trying to pick up the voices of my people at the bottom of the mountain on the short frequencies, then the signals of exploration ships and then, even further away, the communications between the Middle Kingdom and their orbital stations. I ate alone, slept alone, without fear for my safety but without succeeding in breaking the invisible barrier that persisted between them and me.

Then, on that fourth night, a child came to me and said:

"You have to come and tie the braid."

I was stunned.

"Can you speak my language?

- We need you.

- Why now? How long have you been at it?"

By nightfall, almost the entire community had gathered on a small esplanade behind the hangars. Beasts and men had settled around a large dry coconut fire. The child guided me to them, led me into the light and said:

"Tell us."

THE BRAIDS

Back in port, then on the boat, during the two dozens that it takes to make the return trip, I tried to record from memory the long hours of stories deployed in this tribe of human story-tellers. There are many things missing, often very beautiful, nestled in language imperfections that I have not been able to retain or reproduce in writing.

Storytelling was the only aspiration of this community, and these evenings spent together saying and listening were the culmination of every day spent working. They only kept their tools in working order to free up enough resources and time to do so. Radio and light only served to reread, hear and distinguish the signs of worlds beyond. If they taught all children to read, writing was useless to them. They were only interested in perennial traces if they were the product of otherness.

The preferred and almost systematic form of their storytelling is the braid. A braid is said by at least three different people, i.e. with as many voices, from as many points of view. For my sake, the villagers practiced strand by strand, which consists of talking one after the other to weave the stories only from time to time. However, I have witnessed more complex braids several times, where everyone seemed to be talking together, following divergent lines but always overlapping around a subject, a word, a syllable, an intonation or a silence. From these virtuoso stories, I have brought nothing back, not even a theme, only a confused wonder like the one that can capture us listening to the song of many birds together.

On the first evening, still amazed to have discovered that these humans were talking, I came to sit near the fireplace and, under the attentive gaze of the tribe, pulled the first strand of the braid: the near and the far.

The other braids in which I participated, evening after evening, during my stay, often followed the same structure: I began by speaking, adopting my own gaze, my experience, then the women, men and children of the tribe completed my testimony with stories that always seemed to respond to mine without appearing to espouse their own perception of the world.

It also often seemed to me that, whatever the subject seemed to be, their tales always ended up, in one way or another, talking about the stories themselves. As if these stories of telluric movements and cellular reproduction were mainly metaphors for their shared narratives.

I do not claim to have understood how these people lived, because we were never able to communicate outside the braids, and none of my direct questions were ever answered. Conversations outside storytelling evenings always took on a form that was incomprehensible to me, based on brief gestures and sounds shared with their pets. I heard them grunt like that even in solitude, to address the plants they were growing, in the same way and with the same intensity as with a resident of their hut.

What we consider to be articulated language seemed to be strictly reserved for narrative times, and then it did not spare any abstract or technical terms and borrowings from foreign idioms, mathematical language, computer code. It is also possible that they chose to exclude me from their verbal exchanges, taking care not to articulate speech between them if I could witness it.

The braids compiled in this report were collected from memory and contain only the part that I managed to translate, that is, to understand. I transcribed what I could and discarded what I couldn't. Finally, and above all, my account lacks the diversity of voices and bodies from which these words came out, the variety of characters that the storytellers played in turn.

The identity of these humans seemed very mobile to me and I often confused them in the space of a few hours. Their clothing, gait, posture and intonation were constantly changing. I have not learned the names of any of them, I do not know their exact numbers and I know nothing about how they have survived the disasters. Although I probably would have had the opportunity and was later reproached for it, I did not take with me any of the objects of their daily lives, nor any of the books they had preserved.

In fact, I have failed in all my missions, both as an explorer and as a librarian. However, I remain convinced that I have retained the essential in composing this report: a few grains of sand from a full handle, almost entirely escaped between my fingers.

Before walking back down the hill, having counted that it would only take me one day to reach the ships and my companions, I attacked the southwest wall of the circus, hoping to reach the untouched lands that I had heard them describe in the braid of the organization of the world. Dogs preceded me again, on a frightfully steep path that collapsed under my insecure steps. I stopped halfway to the top, dizzy. There was nothing left there but bare rock.

I retraced my steps.

THE RETURN

During the time that my confinement lasted before I could enter the Greenhouse again, I spent all my sleep periods dreaming of the volcano. The sensations I had experienced up there - the cold biting nights, the touch of the living air on my bare legs - mixed with the invented sensations that awakened in me from participating in the braids, and the sensations recreated on the boat as I tried to put the stories in writing.

When I returned to port, after two dozens spent away, my companions did not appear very curious about what I had experienced. As I was giving an oral report of my expedition for the first time, my +1 interrupted me:

"Save this for the chapters and for the Greenhouse. We now need all the musclepower we have to load the aluminum."

The prospecting of the coastal sites had finally borne fruit and I proved to be more useful as a manoeuvre than for my partial knowledge of an abandoned humanity. To perfect my inadequacy, I had brought nothing back from my stay in the Highlands, neither specimen nor document: I was only heavy with my memories – that is, nothing, an imperceptible change in my own self.

But once restored to the environment that had seen me be born, that had shaped and nourished me as a girl, these evenings spent by the fire listening, talking and listening some more took on an ever greater importance in my mind. I physically recognized the smells, the lights, the feelings of confinement and security of my Greenhouse, but at the same time contemplated these enclosed, narrow and temperate places with a renewed eye.

I had to get used again to the short cycles of our universe and I slept a lot: the cell where I spent my quarantine was filled with old people, pigs, babies, jellyfish and ferns, phosphorescences similar to those emitted by archive projectors, mists, sparkling stars.

As soon as I was again found compatible with the colony, I requested an audience with my +3 and gave her a copy of the report with emotion. Several dozen passed by without my having the slightest news and I ended up getting impatient. I kept talking about the island, the tribe and the braids to my colleagues at work. For them, I mimicked the flight of birds, imitating the raucous sounds of dogs, both less realistically than on the archive tapes we were in charge of. The most polite of my +0s let me get carried away for a while, then they returned to their problems of classification, interface and consultation.

Other expeditions were successfully launched. The explorers of Third Zanzibar were at the forefront of adaptation. It was estimated that the deadline for the recapture of the Outside was in four or five generations maximum. The time was short but it was enough to make this horizon virtual: none of us, none of the children we would know would see the dawn of this new age.

I was finally summoned for an interview. An emergency chapter on the compliance of radiation filters occupied the usual room and I was received in an annex cabinet. It was a narrow and long space, with an entire wall covered by the cardboard floor plan of the lower levels of our Greenhouse. The dusty ventilation was snoring in each of the silences of our painful exchange.

My +3 seemed exasperated by something I couldn't grasp – physical pain, perhaps – and kept her eyes constantly lowered on her notes.

"What type of organization prevails in this society?", she enquired at first. "How do they ensure cohesion, how do they maintain order? Who makes the decisions? Do they have weapons and what use do they make of them?"

I replied that I knew nothing about it. I talked about free-range cattle, flourishing crops. She let me speak for a few minutes and then she took it up again:

"Where do they get their information from? What do they know about the Greenhouses? Who keeps them informed of the spatial progress of the Middle Kingdom? »

I then mentioned the radios, the computer, and admitted that I myself had sometimes told them about my home world. My interlocutor leaned down even lower on her tablet and took long notes, without saying a word.

I could see the white parting on her skull, where her pulled back hair separated. Words came to me, which I kept in my mouth out of deference, out of caution.

It was not their technical means that mattered, I wanted to explain to her, but their attention span. They had organized themselves to be able to tell, and that meant, at first, listening carefully to everything. The gestures, the mimics, the waves, the words: nothing the world said seemed insignificant to them.

"What do they have that we don't?" the woman asked me, this time raising her wet eyes towards me.

I hesitated to answer her frankly, but she followed:

"How did they survive on the Outside? Did you bring back any genetic samples? Any objects that some of them may have manipulated?

- No, I confessed. Nothing at all."

I mentioned the purification procedures, upon my return, the simplicity of their way of life, the slightness and the importance in their eyes of documentary collections. She nodded, put away her stylus and contemplated her hands.

We were sitting at a small table across from each other. I could have touched her by reaching out, by leaning over a little, but I felt like there was a huge distance between us.

She said:

"You can return to your position, file your report in its place and resume your usual work. Your exploration mission is over."

I didn't answer anything. There was one voice missing from this exchange. Our two monologues collided without meeting and the whispering of the air in a closed circuit only produced a low parasitic noise. It seemed to me that an impossible insect was moving away, at the edge of my field of vision, but I did not turn my head towards it, for fear of making it disappear.

STORIES
COLLECTED

BRAID
[OF NEAR AND FAR]

VOICE 1

I was born twenty-three years ago in the coastal greenhouse of Third Zanzibar, capital of the southern district, from the belly of a healthy volunteer and the encounter of selected and corrected gametes for maximum compatibility with the environments of the Outside.

I belong to the eighth generation of explorers of my Greenhouse, the twelfth in the world network, and I hope for the future of the entire human community that we are among the last. I hope that the time will soon come for us to reconnect with the Outside, to forget crises, epidemics and wars, and to rebuild relationships with all human beings, those in space and those, like you, who have survived tragedies, sheltered in the folds of the world, with courage and tenacity.

As a girl, I was a dreamy and clumsy apprentice, unable to develop a passion for behavioural teaching and not very good at technical work. However, I could spend hours in the archives and see the same old health and safety clips ten, twenty times over:

the ones for the children and then all the others, those containing images of the past, reconstructions. The fires were my favourite, so shiny and monstrous, and the drones' zooms that suddenly changed the scale of the landscapes, revealing both the scale of the disaster and the immenseness of the Outside.

Then, when I was old enough, I spent all my leisure segments in the Greenhouse library, consulting visual and sound documentation, reading digitized books, discovering and inventing the delirious variety of the worlds before. Thanks to these files, I learned the basics of about twenty languages. From the age of sixteen, I started to participate in the loading of communication containers between Greenhouses. The reports and protocols were no secret to me and I exchanged by radio with colleagues in neighbouring districts. I was a data compiler trapped in a three-star explorer's body.

I've never liked martial training, I'm unable to empty a magazine into a fixed target. I had to convince my +3s of the usefulness of enrolling me as a librarian, of the need to find the books missing from our knowledge of the world, of my ability to sort out the wheat from the chaff on the spot, of my ability to make contact with possible survivors.

The idea of the Outside turned me on and terrified me equally. What I dreamed of, when I boarded the ship, was to see the visions of my childhood recordings recreated in space. I had no idea, however, of the feeling of immensity and danger that would grip me, along with an impression of nudity, loneliness and fragility.

A fire capable of turning the night itself red is neither an image nor a story: it is my end in person. I didn't know what fear was, behind the word itself.

I came here for the books and data, for those traces of the age of concrete that you have that are missing from our collection. I came here so that we can refine our analyses, perfect our species and find ourselves here in a few decades, to repopulate the Earth.

In the Greenhouses, we live in an environment of walls and ceilings, glass screens, plastic tents, hutches, silos, dormitories, machines, cold rooms, operating rooms and crematories. We have relationships with the Greenhouses of the South District and the East Coast, and so from one place to another, all around the world.

We form, with our possessions, with our bodies, the archipelago of survivors.

.

VOICE 2

I was born three million years ago, at the end of an unthinkable incubation period, spawned by the heavy darkness that unfolds in the heart of the Earth.

I was born of a burning spurt, a tear and an explosion;
I emerged through the thin film of salt water that bathes the Earth, cooling, freezing as I passed by, but without the need to emerge extinguishing in me. I formed a tumulus, a mole's burrow, then a cone of rock, and this higher and higher, always spitting, always vomiting myself, always petrifying myself, lifting myself up on a new and fresh base. I wanted the light first. Then I went to attack the sky.

I stretched, laid down. The movement in me had the angry and joyful force of life. I was a huge lava surge and I felt boundless. Nothing could have stopped me from reaching the sun, the stars, I was burning, then I was burning less, I became exhausted, I went out.

I knew I had reached adulthood when my crater, too inactive, collapsed on itself. I was then covered with forests and water ran down my sides, cyclones sanded my slopes, animals had come, butterflies that are like flowers and corals that are like rocks.

Another, younger, volcano emerged at my side to relegate me to the rank of ancestors. He was like me two and a half million years earlier, and reminded me of what I had once done. I didn't flinch much anymore. The magma in me had thickened, my pulse had slowed, I had traded my gecko heart for a tamarind heart. When winter came back, I would cover myself with frost and let myself freeze. The snow, which fell on my highest peaks, reflected the moon: it reflected the scale of my endeavour and the size I had achieved.

I watched my neighbour burn, his lava dripping, smoking as it met the ocean, I watched the island grow, which was like myself, and let it grow, just as I let the elements soften me and lower me, let life grow and settle upon me. The times of the furious stone were coming to an end. I fell asleep: from yellow to red, from red to black and from black to grey burned ashes.

I knew my first men only two thousand years ago. They were just passing through, contemplating me from afar. Ten centuries later, they dared to climb on top of me. Another five hundred years and they settled permanently. And the reason I talk about them is because they made a difference here. It is because with them, more than with any mollusc, bird, bacteria or fish, came multitudes of new species, invited from their boats, their clothes, their skins and their entrails. And the changes they made were as numerous and spectacular as those I had been able to make myself in my time.

They were tiny and pale, frenetic. They lived their lives in the space of a sigh, but were populous and fertile, cunning. They came and went as they pleased, touched everything, tasted everything, laughed. I recognized myself in them, as in the neighbouring volcano: they were my peers, with this joyful force, this angry force, indifferent to the consequences, destructive, creative.

And, just as under my air of great sleepiness I am forever at work, so do slowed down humans retain their primitive dynamism.

What has collapsed does not reform itself. It is in the ruins themselves that the living persist.

VOICE 3

I was born a few hours ago, from the death of my mother, and I too will soon die giving birth.

At each step we split ourselves: from one I will become two, just as I became one when I separated from my twin. As long as positive signals are emitted, as long as the neighbourhood is favourable, our lineage will continue to split, act, live and die. To be and to cease to be is the only way we know how to persist, the only thing that keeps life in motion.

I will grow up and move, work, breathe. My existence will be my function, determined by my form, my geographical position and my specialization. I will do as my mother did before me, as my daughters will do after my division. I will not transform myself: I will be transformation myself.

At the end of my existence, my informational content will first duplicate itself. My chromatids will attach from the middle to their brand new copies, while I will grow, swell up to twice my usual size. The organelles essential to my functioning that I shelter in my bosom will also take this opportunity to be doubled, to be able to accompany my two unborn daughters.

Once all these preparations are completed, my chromosomes will compact, condense, become huge, and my nucleus that has housed them until now will break up. The released chromosomes will line up at the equator where, from the poles, protein filaments will launch themselves to grab them, pull them to either side, and tear them apart until they break at the intersection of their X. The broken chromatid pairs will move away from each other, at each end of my working self. A new envelope will come to wrap them up and it will be the signal of the end. I will split for good, become two, cease to be.

My existence is only meaningful if it is perceived through this system that subsumes me. In space: I do what needs to be done in the place where I am, in interaction with my neighbours, for the benefit of the whole. In time: I am a moment in the chain of subdivision, a part of a story that contains me, a simple sentence, a simple word. The most beautiful part of my life is the part I devote to my duplication. In this work of copying that I aspire to accomplish in the most precise way possible, there are errors, omissions or additions. These artifacts are part of my raison d'être and are not errors: they appear randomly, inserting into the conservation process the subtle chaos of novelty. In some cases, very rarely, these changes have a concrete effect on the functioning of the affected cells. More exceptionally, they have an impact on neighbouring cells, cause a collapse, modify a collaboration, even affect the superstructure in which we exist. Then it may be that I die for real, that I die even in my offspring, pushed to annihilation by this neglect.

At my scale, that of the somatic cell, mutations can only at most affect the individual of which I am an intimate part. But if I were a germ cell, busy matching, recombining, separating chromatids, my mutations would have no impact on my daughter cells. These, carrying the modification, would remain incapable of reproducing without the encounter of another gamete, outside our superstructure.

It is in this new individual that the mutation would unfold, beneficial or harmful, perhaps neutral, requiring a change of perspective, a new scale, a step backward to be understood, to be perceived.

BRAID
[OF THE FORMS OF HUMANITY]

VOICE 1

We are the inhabitants of the Greenhouses. We are the human race.

We have survived climate change, increased concentrations of carbon dioxide and methane in the atmosphere, natural and human disasters, collapsing animal populations, recombinant and melted permafrost ice viruses, wars over arable land, access to fresh water, control of military bases, knowledge centres and symbolic places. We have created havens and allowed our world to continue. These sites are at the same time bunkers, laboratories and utopian cities, they are like these drawings in medieval manuscripts representing the worlds nested into each other, all similar on different scales: the cosmos, the city, man himself.

We designed a total of one hundred and eleven Greenhouses, distributed all around the world according to material capacities and population densities. They were planned, financed and built with the support of what remained of international organizations, peacekeeping forces and universities. They are the last testimony to the universalism that once guided mankind: a science without borders, a unity of destiny for the human species, a responsibility towards its environment.

We populated the Greenhouses with animals of which we had sufficiently varied specimens and genetic strains. We planted the crops we needed and stored the seeds of those we could use later. We organized our islets into a closed network of intelligences, populated with the same scientific rigour that has presided over our entire program, creating this skilfully controlled archipelago in which to live and make people live while waiting to reclaim the troubled Outside. We defended these bastions against the attacks of the outcasts and showed great rigour in everything, because the common good was on our side. Because we were the last hope of our entire species and the conservators of biodiversity.

We lived under the domes of our Greenhouses despite the fact that our initial project was not completed. As our hybridization capacity progressed, we produced mutants that were able to better adapt to the Outside. We, the children of the Greenhouses, will soon be able to re-acclimatise livestock and farmed fish on Earth. We will be able to travel from Greenhouse to Greenhouse, to meet the cousins we have only connected with over the years through radio waves. On a reset planet, purged of billions of people swept away by the crises, we will resume the course of the human adventure. We will continue its work, which is based on the accumulation of knowledge and an ability to constantly increase our influence.

We will be benevolent this time, enriched by our mistakes, softened by the catastrophe that almost killed us. The principles of sharing, reason and responsibility will guide our facilities. And to our children, we will teach the history of the Greenhouses, these monumental arks, which have managed, despite the chaos, to preserve fragments of this unchanging world strictly arranged by our genius.

VOICE 2

We are the Homo sapiens virginalis. *We are the human race.*

We were born fifteen generations ago from the womb of our last ancestor, sapiens sapiens. *The name of this genitrix is no longer known to us, but we hope she lived happily and we will always remember her with emotion and a touch of embarrassment. We only knew the Earth a few years before we were sent to the Station, where we began to reproduce.*

From mother to daughter, we are named Nora. Our species is made up of a single she-individual who reproduces herself indefinitely. In the absence of drug treatments, we become pregnant on our own at the age of twelve years and four months, then every ten and a half months, on a regular basis, until menopause. However, we prefer to draw off the zygotes before the beginning of their segmentation and work to improve them. We then store these possible filiations and select the most interesting ones before shipping them in capsules to the extrasolar planets.

We are still forced to embark on a liferaft : a pubescent Nora, kept asleep in a kind of coffin. Soon, however, we will have made enough progress to use artificial uteri and synthetic placentas.

Space and resources are limited in the Station, so few of us are born, and even fewer reach nubile age. Nevertheless, we are innumerable because all of us, gametes, embryos, daughters, mothers, engineers, technicians, pilots, are aware that we are one family, one race, one species, whether we are gathered or dispersed, conscious or dormant, orbiting the Earth or drifting beyond the limits of the solar system.

This world we have left is nothing more than a set of colourful spots in the Station's windows. A piece of landscape brighter than the sky, unpleasantly mobile with its varying cloud patterns. We can hear the radios still emitting below and understand the growls of the sapiens rising from the bottom of their prison. Sometimes we feel compassion for them, we wish them to succeed in their turn to free themselves from the earth's attraction, to free themselves from mud, dust and rot. To come closer to us, deep down: to become their own universe and no longer depend on anything but themselves. To only rely on their own minds, on their ability to improve, adapt and survive in unknown environments that are still unimaginable.

Most of the time, however, we look elsewhere. The blinking of the stars articulates a signal that is addressed to us. We cut off the receivers to talk only to each other, from one Nora to another. We perform calculations, conduct experiments, calibrate the rations of our own milk, our own meat. We study, breed and hybridize the beings we are hosts to and with whom we live in good harmony, acarids, bacteria, archaeas, viruses.

We are Nora and each of us lives in their body like a space capsule thrown across time and space. We are Nora, all connected to each other, and forever cut off from the Earth that has nurtured us, kept us in childhood, finally allowed us to emancipate ourselves.

VOICE 3

We are the inhabitants of the Highlands. We are the human race. We live together like the myxomycetes, sing like the tec-tec, fly like the tec-tec when we watch it fly. We have the eyes of the dogfish and the eyes of the octopus, the eyes of the babook. We grew from a seed like filao and rose towards the sky like medlar wood, like the chayote. Like the screw pine, we grow with more joy when we are in company, when benevolent beings raise us but do not manipulate us too much. We are the humanity born from the eyes of dogs, cats, pigs, palms, stones, mosses and earthworms, light and wind, and under the touch of rain which is what we have in us most human.

We are the humanity that listens as much as it can, that exists in its capacity for attention. We listen to the sounds of animated and inert things, to the sounds of well-drawn and fuzzy things, and to all silences, and to all signals sent by gestures. We are the humanity that constantly exchanges between itself and with the world, the humanity of the skin, of the imagination, of the mobile border.

We have collected some of the knowledge of those who were before us and have carefully transmitted their ability to understand and be amazed. Their knowledge was beautiful and strange, and we can only admire the turn of mind that governed their accumulation, and can only shudder at the blindness they testify. They repeat a fascinating history, a terrible mythology, a grandiose aspiration. Because we know how it ended, we feel the tragedy of that enthusiasm for knowledge.

We know what distinguishes us from non-human beings, and we know that this is where our responsibility as a species lies: the ability to tell stories.

We are human because we know how to say I am a herb-Robert, I am a boletus, I am a dream herb, I am this ylang-ylang flower and this mist, I am this flame, I am this beetle when it was larva, I am this dead parent when it was a child, I am this desire, I am the memory of this desire and this way of telling the story.

We are humanity because we know how to capture in the net of words what the rest of the universe expresses, by connecting our meagre catches, the little bit of what we manage to retain, and because we can witness what is no longer as well as what is not yet.

We are humanity because we have accepted this task of articulating and transmitting, of listening in order to hear, of translating, of lending a voice to the world, rather than claiming that what is not audible is silent and that what is silent is not us.

The water flows better than we do. The weeds are more patient. The cow dreams more deeply. The rock casts unparalleled shadows. Everyone does what they can.

What we do is tell the story.

BRAID
[OF KNOWLEDGE AND IGNORANCE]

VOICE 1

I am the water mill.

I stand at the edge of the village, between dwellings and plantations, halfway between the library and the huts, on the border between the worlds of animals and plants. Each of the parts I am made of have been manufactured, modified and improved in order to optimize my smooth running as a whole. I was desired for my function, I was dreamed up and shaped for it. I am in the world to produce electricity by taking advantage of the constant flow of our water spring without taking a drop of it, without impairing crop irrigation or the village's supply. For as long as I can remember, the spring has been falling from the heights with the same stubborn energy, the same joyful power. She sings as she approaches, rushes with air, throttles into the penstock, then jumps shuddering out of the nozzle and crashes into me, pushing my wheel.

The blades of my turbine are hollow. They look like alignments of bowls, which move back one after the other under the continuous pressure of the flow. A slight offset between the two series, aligned on either side of my wheel, allows me to collect the divided jet at the moment of impact. Day or night, whether the weather is dry or pouring rain, whether the earth roars or is covered by early morning frost, my wheel moves, perfectly balanced, it rotates without play around the axis in a vast but almost invisible movement, without ever advancing, without ever retreating. If you look at me long enough, you can almost think of me as motionless, balanced, with no past or future. In other words: timeless. Sometimes I slow down, however, or accelerate. And of course, I continuously deteriorate. I have been stopped, sometimes, to change one of my parts that has become fragile or defective.

As long as my wheel rotates, it drives this rod, called a shaft, which is my axis of rotation. And the shaft, in turn, rotates the permanent magnet attached to it inside the fixed tube of the solenoid. In the large fixed coil of conductor wires, the rotating magnetic field of the rotor induces the electric current, which is my product. This electricity supplies the lamps, radios and computers in the library, the tools in the electronics laboratory. Sometimes, too, this power is only used for the pleasure of producing artificial sounds, useless and beautiful lighting. Or else, my current is produced in pure waste and immediately wasted, a vain corpuscular excitation in a few meters of twisted copper cables.

Through simple and carefully manufactured tools, I change the flow of water into energy, and this process requires only a little attention to my proper operation and maintenance. Thanks to me, the work of the world generates comfort and joy.

Each of my parts has been manufactured. My moving parts are lubricated, those that are sensitive to cold and heat are protected, all my signs of fatigue are monitored. My conductive networks are maintained, my electrical power distribution system is controlled. My inventors know enough about electromagnetism to frame and understand what I am.

It is my magnet, my rotation and my coil that together make this electricity which is not, in its nature, any different from the one that falls from the sky and that you call lightning, or from the one that circulates in the fibers of your being and that you call nervous impulses. My electricity only differs from these wild electricities in the form you have given it and the purpose you have set for it.

I am made of carved wood and metals, I am made of carbon, like you, of iron, like the earth's core, of copper, like the stones on the surface, and of long, carefully shaped fabric sheaths. I am made with intelligence and love to serve a purpose.

I remain unique in my village, because I serve little purpose. What needs would there be for more household energy? For everything else there are your arms, your number, all the powers of the universe.

VOICE 2

I am the water.

I am liquid. I flow, I expand, I mingle and warm up. All the voices in the world are mine. You can hear me everywhere, falling and gurgling, crackling. I boil in the pan, evaporate, condense against the lid and fall back into the flame.

Wherever I lie, on the surface, in the puddles and on the leaves, in the immense and shimmering spaces of the seas, I surrender myself to the caress of the sun's rays. Heated, I evaporate, I become gaseous to mix with the ambient air. I disguise myself to blend in, become almost invisible, barely tangible, a touch, a tiny drop formed at the end of a hair, a ghost of mist on the horizon. I rise, condense and adorn myself with a thousand shades of white, grey, black, and with the infinite new shapes that your eyes lend me. I get carried away here and there, as if I were a colony of migratory birds or a jellyfish pulled by the backwash. I vibrate and move under the twists of the wind, I hold back, I release the light, I become purple and gold and green, why not, explode through the sky the spectrum of light into multicolored crowns. I form colossal towers, carpets and swollen monsters, shred or unravel, wind up into a cyclone if necessary, charge up with lightning.

I burst into rain. I fall, crystallise into flakes, fall as liquid, the water in the water makes circles, millions, billions of impacts immediately erased, and on the submerged land of craters, ponds, streams. I seep into soft ground, I furrow hard ground. I pull out the best planted trees, drown the heaviest beasts. I sweep away your best masonry structures in an instant.

I am the waterfall and the glacier. I am in the pitcher to which you quench your thirst, and like all parts of the universe, I only aspire to stability, which is the other name for chaos. I know that when nothing holds me back anymore, when I am able to go anywhere I want because I have used, softened, liquefied every obstacle, then there will be no difference between me and myself, and everything will be finished.

I am everywhere around you, from the closest to the most distant, in your blood and the tissue of your lungs, your brain, your muscles. In everything you ingest and in everything you eliminate, in lettuce and shit. I'm on your breath. I am in your kisses and in your tears.

Down to the deepest layers of the Earth's mantle lie primordial waters, which remain liquid under the pressure of surrounding rocks. Sometimes fragments of these wet stones rise to the surface, forming incredibly strong kinds of eggs, mineral drops whose contents, as soon as revealed, evaporate in a whisper. Across space drift tremendous clouds of hydrogen and water, like those that once caressed our Earth, those that gave it its present face.

I am everything: what is swarming around you, what is growing, what is watching you, what looks like you. I make up for most of the weight of the cells of all living organisms. Everything that lives, thus, is similar, because ultimately you are nothing but pockets of water in pockets of water. I am everywhere above, everywhere below and always around you. I cover two thirds of the planet's surface. I absorb almost all of the far infrared rays into the atmosphere. I can turn off the sun in your eyes. I cool and silence the volcano, turn its drool into rock, its fire into smoke, its rage into resentment. I keep you on the island and protect you from visitors. Wherever I am, I am incapable of limiting myself: life within continues to flourish, from the sparkling surface of the oceans to the darkest, most confined of the underwater depths. Algae, gametes, larvae and micro-organisms form a slurry of carbon and living water mixed with dead water, an intangible fauna and flora, vaguely opaque, a submerged cloud split by the long body, the denticulated skin of the tiger shark.

You lean over the soothed water of your bowl to contemplate what has appeared on the lens that forms my surface. You see yourself in me like in a dark mirror, and a fragment of the world cut out behind you. Come closer again. Your face fills the circle, your eye in the center.

I'm also in the liquid that moistens your cornea: your mirror in that mirror.

VOICE 3

I am the mystery.

I am the laughter of the very young child, anxious and then relieved. The adult leans towards it. Smile. Smile. Then it hides its face behind a cloth or with its hands. This only lasts for a moment. When it reveals its face again with a joyful little noise, the child jumps before laughing. It laughs because what has just happened is magical and all the more wonderful that it is happening again at will. This person it looks at, whom it loves, whom it conceives in their eternity, plays at ceasing to exist and then returning to the world.

Where did they go? Where did they go? What is this place made of where the things that have disappeared persist? And how can we be sure that they will be able to come back once again, once more?

I am the shadow without a body.

I am the dragon.

I am the word thing.

I am that idea you had in your dream, which you remembered once and then forgot. Many years later, you found me in a different dream and recognized me. Before you forgot me again, you had time to ask yourself: was I one and the same idea? Did you invent me at every opportunity or only the second time? What did you remember? The idea itself or the memory of the idea? Or had I only been two different reflections of a third idea that was forever unknowable?

I am what the young corn shoot, the old cardinal passerine, and your heart desire when the grey dawn comes. I am what you count beyond your tenth finger, what you conceive beyond this hour that begins, what you believe is waiting for you behind the closed door.

I am the pleasure you feel in advancing inside me, your little domesticated flame raised at arm's length, in order to illuminate as far as possible in my darkness. It is not only the satisfaction of victory, the satisfaction of seeing me retreat under the effect of your intelligence, the pride of knowing that you are a little more powerful than yesterday. It is also the simple joy of setting foot on a still new ground, a renewed ground, like a footprint in the virgin snow. And It Is also the complex joy of knowing that this knowledge is nothing in itself, and that my darkness extends beyond all your exploration abilities.

I am all the unanswered questions and all the questions you don't think to ask yourself.

Do you know how to dress without raising silkworms?

Do you know how to feed yourself without working the land?

Do you know how to be quiet without having to fight?

And then I am also, I am especially, in each of the folds of what you think you know, hidden behind each of these things that you think you understand. I am in the water and in its cycle, in its appearance on Earth of which you know almost nothing, in the randomness of its movements, small and large, in the unpredictability of its transformations. I am in the cloud that will stay there or pass by, that will give rain or disperse in the air, that will make people live or that will kill. I am in the mill, whose malfunction you can anticipate without being able to predict it, and I am in the electricity it produces, which you can measure without being able to contemplate, feel, understand or tell it. I am in the sense of the words you hear spoken during the braid, in the calls of the animals close to you when they are hungry, when they are afraid or when they just want to play, I am in the modulations of the newborns' crying and in your ability to feel the intention they convey.

You have only taken three steps forward into the depths of darkness and you already feel like you have conquered an entire kingdom. This meagre space, because you cleared it yourself, you claim to call it yours and have power over it. But suddenly, a blessed memory comes back to you, and you are seized with nostalgia for the place where you were before. So you turn around to retrace your steps and suddenly realize that the universe behind you was as dark as the one you were heading into.

For a moment you see the measure of the mystery, the unthinkable sum of everything you ignore that you ignore.

BRAID
[OF SAVAGE AND THE DOMESTIC]

VOICE 1

We have no memory of that time when we didn't go dressed and standing. In the same way, we have not kept a memory of the time when you were not running beside us, hairy, on all fours. Untiring travellers, we have never stopped moving forward, sometimes in front of us, sometimes behind us: our tracks and yours are merging.

In ancient times, wolves lived in the distance, in red and underground worlds, illuminated by uncontrollable fires, or in the last heights of steep mountains where stone turns into ice, and sometimes even beyond peat bogs, in the dark humidity of coniferous forests. Those who were our ancestors did not approach them and they avoided us in the same way, so that they would never meet each other except in a dream or during a visionary trance. We called wolf the fear that seized our children when they woke up at night, and wolf the man's face when he came out of himself to commit despicable acts.

One evening, after spending the day picking shellfish by a lake, returning to the camp weighed down by her basket and the child she was carrying in her belly, a woman turned around on the way and saw the wolf following her from afar. He made no noise, advanced alone, did not seek to attack or hide from her. So the woman did not drive him away and, when she reached home, when she settled in the light and warmth, in the voice sounds of her relatives, she turned around again to see the dozens of yellow eyes that shone beyond the circle of light and the boundaries of the village.

Another story tells that it happened in the early morning, after a night of stalking, and that it was the wolf that surprised the man, leaping before him on the buffalo they were after. The two hunters were so surprised to discover each other that they let their prey escape. And then it was man who chose to follow the beast to its own den. The man who, fascinated by his discovery, then brought in the members of his own family. Wolves, she-wolves and cubs shared with our ancestors the same landscapes, the same perfumes, the same foods.

Both of these stories say only one thing: we do not remember the time when we were not side by side. And maybe there was never any such moment of the meeting. I affirm that all that matters are these centuries spent together, these common worlds travelled and sniffed out, these nights populated by our cries, these meadows and caves, these ice deserts, which today fill our memories and our imaginations.

We took in your motherless cubs and raised them. You saved our children from warthogs, pumas and bears. We skinned your corpses to walk under the cover of your skins. You ate the bodies of those of us who had succumbed to the cold. You taught us how to run. We taught you how to play. You shared what you knew: invisible paths, silent walking, the faces of the moon. We removed the thorn from your paw and cleaned your wounds. You bit the hand that fed you. We removed the splinter that called for our touch.

During all this time of proximity, man and wolf have been transformed. It was a change invisible to the eye, as delicate as the face of the mother in the face of the daughter, or the stories between the story we were hearing and the one we were retelling. But man, like the wolf, changed his appearance and size and behaviour. When he stopped biting at every turn, his teeth shrank, his face lightened up, his voice calmed down. He began to make love whenever he wanted and not only in periods of rut. He preferred to resolve his conflicts through play rather than physical confrontation. Throughout his life, he retained within him the passions and attitudes of the youthful age.

And it all went so well that one day, the wolf who lived with the man came to see him and said to him: I am no longer as I was before, this wolf who lives beyond you, in the wild worlds. I am your cousin, your brother and your best friend, so similar to you that now I have to answer a new name. So the man named him: dog.

Then the man confessed: I too am no longer the same, but I have no idea what happened to the one who grew up without you, and I am unable to invent a new name for myself, so please tell me, how can I call myself?

The dog did not answer and, since that day, has reserved its answer.

Through the dog, we became human.

VOICE 2

In the dish, on the fire, the rice is cooking. The water snores, translucent and a little sticky. The steam rises with the scent of meals, the promise of shared food. Then, under the lid and the cloth, the drained rice rests for a moment in its own humours. It awaits our hands and appetites, a white dune, a block that our fingers crumble. The long, waterlogged grains, soft, resist a little bit under the tooth. Rice brings us together.

From one meal to another, it keeps us alive, from this day to the next. We remove the bran and germ, steam it and store it in large ceramic vessels, glass jars, plastic pots, when we decide to stay in the same place for several years or centuries. We keep the grain inside in its hull and in large baskets, when we prefer to go from one place to another during the same life.

Wherever we settle, we bring its seeds with us: a few handfuls of grains saved from the reserves that we replant where we stop. Rain rice, puddle rice, flood rice. We build water reservoirs, dikes and canals not far from our shelters. Abundantly watered, the stem grows stiff and high. It carries the new grains that we harvest and, for some, put back into the soil. We can replant the rice up to three times a year.

Around the villages, the flooded fields are jade green and we move around, up to our knees in water. We then reflect ourselves, creatures without feet, with four arms, two opposite heads, armed with double sickles. The grass we cut seems to have two heavy seed buds and grow without roots, as if in the open sky. It no longer looks like a plant, this rice we grow, but like a manna torn from the world above, a concentrate of life in its greenness, folded in its hulk, a fragment of our existence, of the effort of our muscles.

We remember the days when rice was a weed, a stiff plant of wet meadows and swamps, so densely planted that it prevented herds from grazing, boats from passing through. We would watch the sparrow pecking at the fallen grains that had not rotted and mock its diet, its tiny appetite, its low standards. But we also envied it for knowing how to feed on this negligible plant. For being able to survive wherever it decided to land after a day of strolling through the air.

At that time, we already had the rope, the spade and the oar. We had been living with the boar for so long that it had become a pig like us, and had been living with the buffalo for so long that it had become a draught animal like us. We made sculptures, dyes, jewellery. So we also took wild rice, this red rice with small and scarce seeds, this lazy rice, with a long sleep and a bland taste. And this rice, in turn, took us with it.

It taught us to look at it, feel it, taste it. It showed us what it loved and feared, taught us to handle, support and respect it. At each harvest, as we became wiser and closer to it, its grains lengthened and its taste changed. We brought it along here and there, we fattened or thinned it, pampered or neglected it. And in turn, it satisfied or punished us, its crops went bad, it attracted parasites, turned bitter. We chose and replanted the one that yielded the best, again, and again. And it elected those of us who digested its starch best, again, and again.

Our children, fed regularly, have lived longer. Our camps have grown. We have established larger rice fields, and the grain has lost its ability to spread. We have built dams, tanks, supply networks, planted and harvested more and more quickly, and the dormancy phase of the seeds has decreased. We have gained in physical strength, endurance, number, and each plant has multiplied the number of its seeds, and each seed has gained in size.

But just as well, we can tell this story the other way: it is by securing this food source, by protecting the production from variations between dry and rainy seasons, by making it more abundant and tasty, that rice has made us sedentary, farsighted, healthy and gourmet.

This time we spent together has transformed us beyond what we can imagine. To say of the man that he invented agriculture is like stopping halfway through the story, saying only half a sentence, only the beginning of a word.

Beneath the surface of the rice field, bare feet sink. They touch the soil in which the rice has taken root. The bird that looks down from the sky cannot see this, but it still knows: even it returns to the earth from time to time.

Through rice, we became human.

VOICE 3

For a long time, we pretended to believe that we were the only ones capable of words.

Until the age of concrete, mother, father, family and friends would look down at the newly born child and say: just as we made you in our image, we will teach you our words. By their power, you will become master of the stories and give things, animals, plants and ideas their true name. You will say them and transmit a truth about them. To thank you for prolonging our existence beyond our own death, we give you this power and make you, in turn, a master of language.

Over the hundreds of generations that this age lasted, men have narrated every single thing they made, as well as as as many as possible of the living things, chlorobions, zoobions, fungi, cnidarians, sponges, and everything they could grasp about the invisible and abstract world, and they have used these words as if they were only addressing themselves, turning what they were talking about into characters, sounds, signs. All this time, they pretended not to understand that what they were talking about was addressed to them at the same time. That they were never alone with their stories. That the stories made them as much as they made the stories.

When that age ended, when we finally realized that we were not kings and not even benevolent mothers, but only a tiny part of this world, then we admitted that, in our language, what we were talking about was talking back to us. That what we described in these natural stories was ourselves describing what we thought was the world. And that our ability to articulate was not for us alone, but for the totality of what exists and does not exist.

We began to transform our stories and our stories began to transform us.

Through storytelling, we became human.

BRAID [OF ALL IMMORTALITIES]'

VOICE 1

We, the Greenhouse survivors, have defied death.

It has taken us tens of thousands of years of effort, thousands of generations and the construction of incredibly effective and complex communication systems. We had to invent the coloured pigment, the firing of ceramics, the cart and the boat, the sextant, the bitumen, the pulp, the domestic pigeon, the artificial satellite, the optical fibre. It was necessary to map wilderness areas, underground networks, summits and abysses. We had to improve our teaching and learning techniques. This great work required glossaries, indexes, encyclopedias and atlases. The entire universe has been traversed and described, has been captured, has been transmitted.

It took enormous efforts and huge resources from us, but we finally understood. We now know how the world works, we have become familiar with its organizational principles, with the forces that move it from the subatomic to the cosmic scale. We distinguish between what is beneficial and what is harmful to it. This knowledge of good and evil is both an achievement and a burden. As masters and owners of nature, we are also its guardians and responsible parties.

In this respect, we acknowledge that we are the only ones responsible for the disasters that have occurred. And we will not rest until the time comes to leave the Greenhouses and return to live outside, to repair the wrongs once committed by our ancestors, out of greed, ignorance and a taste for control.

Nature, as we now know, is unpredictable and spontaneous. We will plan our spontaneity.

Individually, we remain fragile, stunted creatures, bounded in tiny space-time. The strength of our arms, the ability of our legs to carry us far away is nothing compared to the size and weight of what is. But an unlimited power is deployed in our organizational capacity, beyond the mountains, seas and abysses of generations. We are invincible because we are countless. The sum of intelligences of our species collected, preserved, completed, updated, allows us to feed and heal ourselves, to entertain and rejoice in all serenity. We have the keys to the world, the sum of all the thoughts, calculations, data and deductions of the humans who preceded us. Our cautious actions also foreshadow the great movements of our descendants.

The human work is an endless continuum, never completed, an ascent to perfection. We are libraries, labs, museums, curiosity cabinets, piles of scholarly journals. We are knowledge and we will not die.

There have been dark ages, difficult hours and sometimes very long eclipses. But humanity has never stopped moving forward, even if it meant reinventing its course, retracing its steps to open a new path.

We are the humanity of the Greenhouses, heir to ancient philosophies, Arab scientists, European monks, encyclopedists, positivists. We are the immortal seeds of knowledge, well protected in our pods, waiting to be replanted, to grow, to rise and to flower again on the whole surface of the Earth.

VOICE 2

We, Nora, have defeated death.

Homo sapiens virginalis*: one species per she-individual.*

Nora: the perfect she-individual to found a species.

It is useless to think of man as a mass, a combinatorial of mortal beings, an addition capable of defying, by its number, the vastness of space and time. On the contrary, we are the daughters of a long series of subtractions, exclusions, the fruit of an enlightened and merciless division, begun at the dawn of time and of which we are today the sublime vanguard and the promise of completion.

We have survived all the tragedies, all the changes and all the epidemics. We are the survivors of the Black Death and Malaria, of the Great Pox and HIV, of misery, of famine, of wars, of genocides. We are the granddaughters of irradiated lands, polluted waters, prions. We are the tenth of a percent of the tenth of a percent of individuals adapted to the harshest conditions. We are the flawless super-humanity, free from all default and weakness, the one that has excluded from its midst the asthmatic, the diabetic, those who are short-sighted, the obese, the hesitant, the hypertensive, the schizophrenic, those with chronic, hereditary or only potential conditions, those who were known as fragile, those at risk of becoming so. We have become immortal by excluding all the faulty elements, by keeping only the best and by improving them further.

We have modelled ourselves on the AquAdvantage salmon and the marbled crayfish, the M6410ipro soybean. We have multiplied our chromosome sets and renounced sexual reproduction, eliminating the least reliable and most fragile half of the old species.

We are Nora, humanity without man, that is, without both males and evils. Our features are impeccable and identical, we see each other as a mirror, each the facet of a unique kaleidoscope. We are all ages at once, old women, infants and mothers. By abolishing personality we have become perpetual.

Each of us, however, remains unique. To protect ourselves from any future epidemic risk and develop new traits, we regularly organize our own mutations. Each Nora can then transmit these innovations intact, by getting pregnant by herself, and this to infinity. Thus, by dispersing ourselves among the stars, we are able to start a strain anew from a single one of us, and add to our mastery of time a total domination of space.

It doesn't matter where we are. We are Nora, the first form of life emancipated from any environment, the perfect species, the matter that has become divine. Each of us is an entire universe and knows for any limit only that of our own body. Our symbiotes and parasites change at the same time as we do in order to stay up to date: for them, we are ideally demanding cosmoses. We are lifeboats for the few lucky germs that will survive the collapse of the Earth.

What is below degrades, collapses and perishes. We, at the top, remain invincible, brilliant, sublime.

The world no longer has any control on us.

VOICE 3

We, narratocene humans, have defeated death.

This voice that speaks, in the future, will remain silent. This tongue, these lips will rot, this face will lose its flesh, the bones that make up this skull will disintegrate and all the carbon that composes me will come to mix, in the ground, with that of the rotten coconut and the excrement of the stag. The memory of these features, of this person, of this moment will disappear, like that of these words and like the language with which, this evening, I am articulating. The world will hardly be any different then from that time near us in the past when this braid - these words, this language, this body, this person - did not yet exist. And yet, it would not occur to you to say of this present that brings us together that it is only an unnecessary lapse, a moment of absence, emptiness and death.

We do not care about power, might or performance, about the accumulation of goods and knowledge. While we prefer to be healthy, satiated, dry and warm, we know that we will sometimes experience illness, pain, loss and boredom. We only use our knowledge for calm and joy. For the rest, we are in the world with humility, which is a sweet and swollen word to describe our deliberate and shifting ignorance.

We know that the universe is beyond our scope, that we will not hold back water by closing our fist, that doing nothing is not inaction, that the foreign does not stop at the surface of our skin and that savagery is as much within us as outside.

We are immortal like the butterfly without a mouth, unable to feed, obsessed with the need to reproduce, like the bud, the red palm kernel, the whale, like the sun and prestressed concrete, like plutonium, like the idea of freedom and like Lise Meitner, like the map of public transport in the city of São Paulo, like Babylon, like Atlantis, like the Big Bang and like the log that finishes burning in white and red and bright grey. We are immortal because we take part in the living matter of the universe, and what is in our heads, in our words, in our tales and in our eyes is no different from anything else.

We have no duty because we have no control, but we have a responsibility because of our ability to tell. We are given the task of carrying as far as possible the account of all that is, without sorting out what exists from what could exist and what will never exist.

We are immortal not because our knowledge will survive but because it will fade and give way to something else. We are the humans of the narratocene: slow, powerless, fragile, connected to each other and to all that proliferates around us. We live to speak and lend voice to the spirits, desires, goats and nostocs that are like us, to machines, to the principles of thermo-dynamics, to geological movements, to DNA sequences, to centuries, to music and to death. We are voices, air vibrations, signals emitted, degraded, muffled, we are contradicted, completed, refined and intertwined messages.

We are not saying: we should say that, *we are saying that.*

Because we do not believe we are everything, we know we cannot think everything. So we say only some of the things: the ones that come to us. Since there is nothing universal, each fragment is of equal importance.

And we, no more than anyone else, do not know where things emerge, where they articulate with each other and where they end.

TALE
[WITHOUT BRAID]

In the beginning, stones and plants taught us the language of the wind.
We climbed the mountains, then, we treaded with our feet the fallen leaves of the undergrowth, the dry and yellow grasses of the high meadows, the rain-coloured moraines, and we hauled ourselves onto the highest peaks. Up above we built a fire, danced a dance and sang a song, until the wind, rejoicing in the show, swirled down to us and agreed to answer the questions that made us suffer.
Hundreds of generations passed, and we unlearned what we knew about dancing and singing. Traditions were lost, the old died without passing on their art to the young, the young went out to play ignoring the calls of the old, and the secret movements, the magic words held in silence eventually dissolved, melting like snow in the sun. But we could still go up the mountain, build the fire and call the wind. And in my breaths and its rumblings, in the cracking of the bent trees, in the beating of the fabrics and the conch of our ears, we heard the reassuring words.
Time has not stopped passing. Tools have invaded our space and our imagination, we have learned to breathe underwater, to fly, to store food, to cleanse wounds, to limit madness, to see in darkness, to seize flames in our bare hands. We organized the universe so well that we forgot how fire was built. When we climbed the summit to ask the wind to light up our roads, solve our riddles and disperse our doubts, we had to admit that we had

left behind our deep memory, that we were like children again. Then, the great whirlwinds whispered, and the wind answered us: I have not forgotten you.

Finally, as the new generations succeeded the old ones, we have lost even the path to the mountain. We have misplaced the maps and directions, neglected to look in the right direction from time to time. Perhaps we dug into the sides, into the depths of the massif, perhaps we leveled it by mistake, to take material from it, to build some of these buildings that seemed essential to us. Perhaps we simply destroyed the mountain out of pride, because we could not bear to see it cast a higher shadow on the world than ours. The day we wanted to question the wind, we gathered here and said: we have nothing left of the knowledge of the ancestors and their magic. We no longer know how to sing the song or dance the dance. We no longer know how to build the fire or climb the mountain. All we know is how to tell the story.

And the wind, the wind answered:

shhhh.

www.disvoir.com

ISBN: 978-2-914563-94-9

Printed by

Petro Ofsetas

Lithuania
Europe

August 2019